The Spirit of the Maasai Man

To the nature of the beast and to all those striving
to keep their spirits free.

Barefoot Books
37 West 17th Street
4th Floor East
New York
NY 10011

First published in the United States of America in 2000 by Barefoot Books, Inc.

This book is printed on 100% acid-free paper

Typeset in Officina Sans
Illustrations prepared in biro, acrylics and crayon on white mountboard

Graphic design by Design Principals, England
Color separation by Bright Arts Graphics, Singapore
Printed and bound in Singapore by Tien Wah Press (Pte) Ltd.

1 3 5 7 9 8 6 4 2

U.S. Cataloging-in-Publication Data (Library of Congress Standards)

Berkeley, Laura.
    The spirit of the Maasai man / written and illustrated by Laura Berkeley.—1st ed.
[32]p. : col. ill. ;   cm.
Summary: Locked inside their cages, the zoo animals have given up hope; they can no longer
hear the songs of their homelands. Then one night, the spirit of the Maasai Man appears. As
he hums his haunting songs, a miracle takes place. By subtly examining the timeless ideal of
love, hope and freedom, this book provokes discussion and a sense of optimism.
ISBN 1-902283-74-0
1. Maasai (African people) — Fiction. 2. Animals — Africa — Fiction.
I. Title.
    [E] —dc21 2000 AC CIP

The Spirit of the Maasai Man

WRITTEN AND ILLUSTRATED BY

LAURA BERKELEY

walk
the way of wonder...
Barefoot Books

Foreword

As I read this book and looked at the touching and beautiful illustrations, I too felt freed by the spirit of the Maasai Man.

There are many things in life that we do not really understand, but most of us know there is "something" beyond the world we see and touch and smell, something intangible. We can call it a spirit and we, like the animals in their cages, can be transported in our minds beyond the walls of our houses and school rooms into a world where our souls can be free. Far from pain, far from suffering.

Laura Berkeley, with her special creative gifts, has, through the Maasai Man, introduced us in a most extraordinary and profound way to the idea of communication with animals. We do not always need to touch and to possess. Sometimes all we need to do is to open our minds and hearts. To let our spirit fly.

Virginia McKenna

Virginia McKenna

The spirit of the Maasai Man is the spirit that lives in all of us. It is given many names and is blessed by many sacred rituals. It is the part of us that is touched by Nature and needs to be free to grow.

Look into the eyes of a caged animal and you will see another spirit as special as your own. It is a spirit that is also blessed by its own sacred rituals. It is a spirit that needs to be free to follow the earth-songs of Nature.

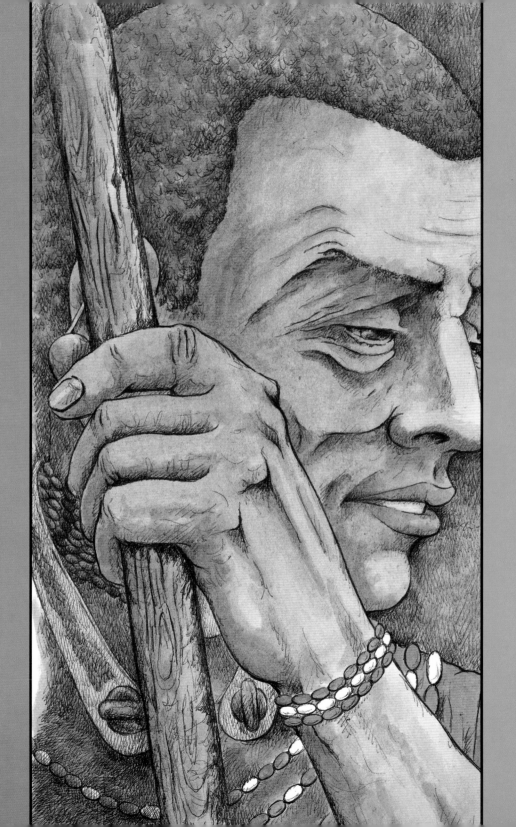

"Why do the zoo beasts cry?"

"Because they cannot hear the songs of the wild," replied the Maasai Man.

Standing at the entrance to the zoo, the spirit of the Maasai Man shimmered in the twilight breeze.

He hummed his haunting earth-songs and the voices of the trapped souls sang out in harmony.

Outside the elephant enclosure, the Maasai Man tapped his stick and in reply a gray shadow trembled in the moonlight.

The Maasai Man sang his song and the spirit of the elephant smelled storm clouds in the air. Silently, she followed the echoes of her herd as it traced its sacred rain-paths across the African plains.

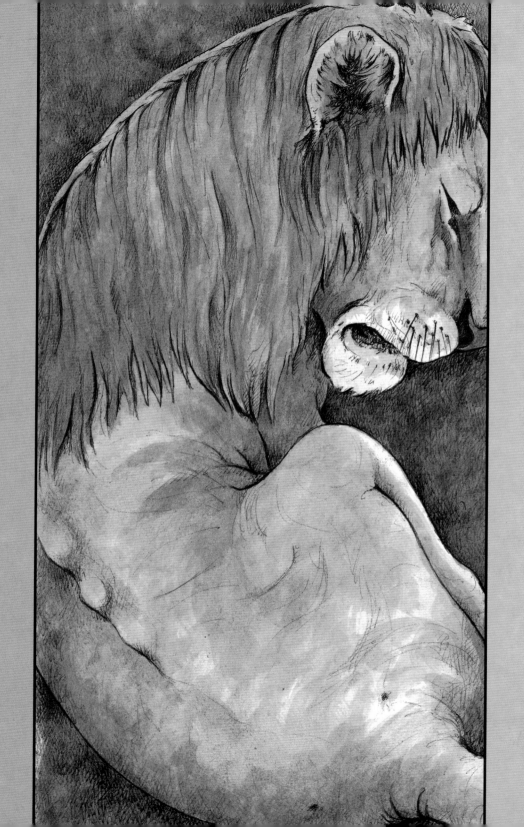

The Maasai Man stopped outside the lion's cage. His eyes grew sad and his song with the lion was long.

The spirit of the lion sat high on his rocky throne and watched, through hooded eyelids, as his kingdom shimmered in the heat of the sun.

Cold and broken upon the concrete floor, the lifeless stripes of the tiger mingled with the bar-shadows of the cage.

The Maasai Man brought down a silver moon and, in the warmth of the Indian night, the spirit of the tiger weaved sinewed pathways through her jungle realm.

The promise of the moon stirred a midnight watcher and she sang to the Maasai Man.

The song was a shadow in the night and the spirit of the wolf ran fast into the cold embrace of a lonely wilderness.

With a face full of wisdom and a hand stronger than man, a noble beast listened to the songs of the Maasai Man.

High in the mountain forests, dark, misty forms gathered around the spirit of the gorilla. With a turn of his hand, he welcomed his family and their wise and gentle ways.

In the dimly-lit corridors of the snake-house, the reflection of the Maasai Man fell upon the coils of the python.

The Maasai song dampened the forest shadows, and the spirit of the python felt the coolness of the rain forest moist against its skin.

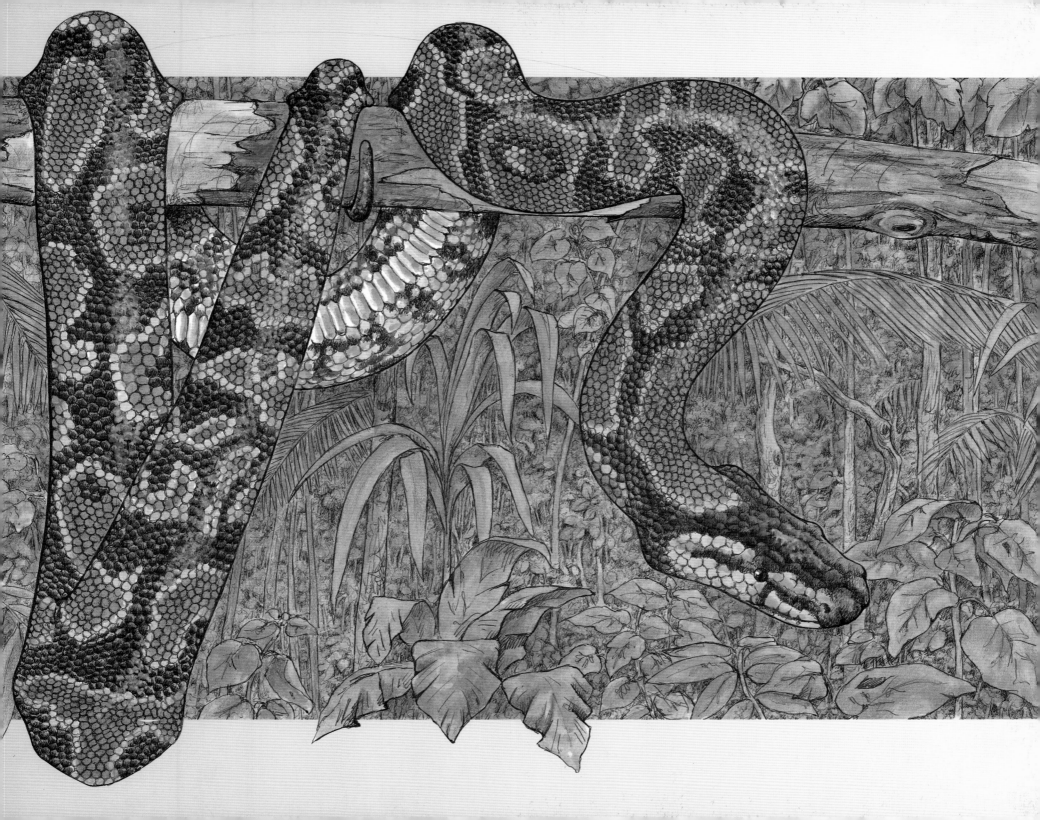

A white sadness sat slumped in the
darkness and the Maasai Man sang
a gentle song.

The spirit of the polar bear could
see the Arctic brightness and,
standing high, touched the frozen
landscape with a longing paw.

The eye of the eagle sees all, and the song of the Maasai Man soared high into the night.

The spirit of the eagle followed the Maasai song to the heights of a mountain ledge and the blueness of the sky unfurled his giant wings.

The Maasai Man sent his songs into a silent concrete world.

Ripples upon the water freed the spirit of the orca and the oceans were filled with whale-song.

All through the night, the Maasai Man sang his songs and the imprisoned beasts felt the freedom of the wild.

The last song lingered with the dawn and, on man's awakening, the animals and the Maasai Man had gone.

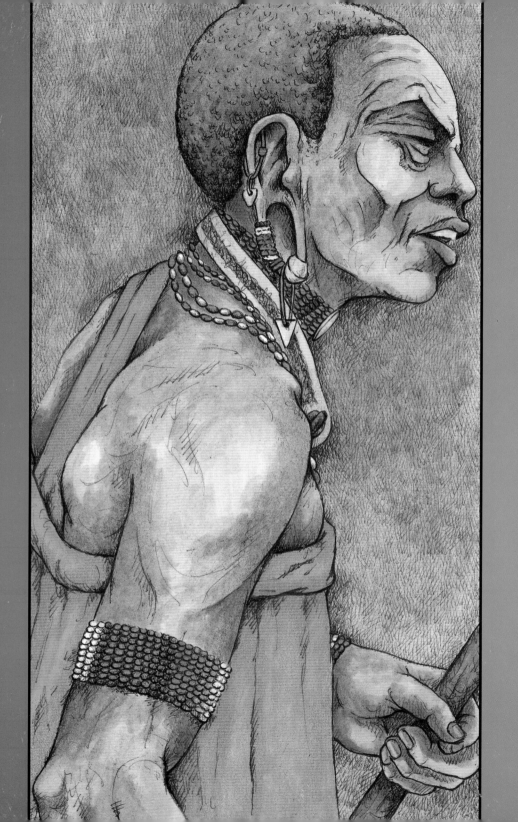

"Why do the beasts sing?"

"Because they are free," replied the Maasai Man.

Author's Note

I have always been fascinated by the images of Africa. The scenery and animals constantly draw my mind and heart to this land of mystery where the human species first rose from the Olduvai Gorge to inhabit the continents of the earth. So it was natural for me to choose the Maasai Man as the main character in this story and the liberator of the imprisoned animals.

Inhabitants of East Africa for thousands of years, the Maasai are one of the last peoples to retain their pastoral culture. The Maasai are named after the language they speak called "Maa." Their way of life is a continuous act of worship to their god, "Engai." They believe that Engai resides on a mountain in the Rift Valley. It was Engai who gave to the Maasai their much-revered cattle; Maasai children are taught to sing songs to the cattle and to recognize each individual cow and bull. At night, the cattle are kept safe in kraals, special circular settlements surrounded by thick fences of thorn-bush to keep out predators such as lions. Inside these kraals, the Maasai build mud huts so that they can sleep close to their animals.
A notable Maasai tradition is that of standing on one leg. To stand on one leg is an act of being still. It is a pose that many aboriginal people adopt, and it serves to remind us that there should be balance in our own lives and that we should have moments of stillness to reflect on our action toward other living beings, human and animal alike.

I wrote and illustrated this book to help bring awareness, and funds, to the important work of the Born Free Foundation. Inspired by Joy and George Adamson during the making of the film *Born Free*, Bill Travers and Virginia McKenna were deeply influenced by the philosophy of the Adamsons, who believed that animals should live freely in the wild. Following the tragic death of the elephant Pole Pole at London Zoo in 1983, Bill and Virginia founded Zoo Check, an organization of just six people with a mission to bring public awareness to the unnecessary suffering of animals in captivity and, where possible, to improve the conditions in which the animals are kept. In 1991, Zoo Check was re-named the Born Free Foundation. The foundation has a wide program of conservation projects and seeks to promote a new awareness of the condition of animals in captivity, as well as championing the right of species of all kinds to exist in the wild in a free and natural way.

For further information about the Born Free Foundation, contact:
Born Free Foundation, 3 Grove House, Foundry Lane, Horsham, West Sussex, RH13 5PL, England.
Tel: +44 1403 240170 Fax: +44 1403 327838
E-mail: wildlife@bornfree.org.uk Website: http://www.bornfree.org.uk

A percentage of the author's royalties from the sale of this book will be donated to the Born Free Foundation.

walk
the way of wonder...
Barefoot Books

The barefoot child symbolizes the human being who is in harmony with
the natural world and moves freely across boundaries of many kinds.
Barefoot Books explores this image with a range of high-quality
picture books for children of all ages. We work with artists, writers and
storytellers from many cultures, focusing on themes that encourage
independence of spirit, promote understanding and acceptance of
different traditions, and foster a life-long love of learning.
www.barefoot-books.com